I HERO

# Viking Blood

Steve Barlow and Steve Skidmore
Illustrated by Sonia Leong

## W
### FRANKLIN WATTS
LONDON•SYDNEY

First published in 2007
by Franklin Watts

Text © Steve Barlow and Steve Skidmore 2007
Illustrations © Sonia Leong 2007
Cover design by Jonathan Hair

Franklin Watts
338 Euston Road
London NW1 3BH

Franklin Watts Australia
Level 17/207 Kent Street
Sydney, NSW 2000

A CIP catalogue record for this book
is available from the British Library.

ISBN: 978 0 7496 7665 0

1  3  5  7  9  10  8  6  4  2

Franklin Watts is a division of Hachette Children's Books,
an Hachette Livre UK company.

Decide your own destiny...

This book is not like others you may have read. *You* are the hero of this adventure. It is up to you to make decisions that will affect how the adventure unfolds.

Each section of this book is numbered. At the end of most sections, you will have to make a choice. The choice you make will take you to a different section of the book.

Some of your choices will help you to complete the adventure successfully. But choose carefully, some of your decisions could be fatal!

If you fail, then start the adventure again and learn from your mistake.

If you choose correctly you will succeed in your adventure.

Don't be a zero, be a hero!

It is the age of the Vikings. You are the captain of the trading ship, *Vidar*. You are sailing home to your village after a long voyage. It has been a good one. You have sold your cargo of hides and grain, and are bringing home weapons and pots that will make you a lot of money.

As your ship rounds a headland, one of your crew shouts out, "Captain, come quickly!"

You make your way to the front of your longship and stare towards land. You gasp in horror – all you can see is burnt timber and wrecked houses. Your village has been destroyed!

"Quickly, men!" you shout, "to your oars and row!"

Your crew obey. Pulling hard and fast towards the shore, you soon reach land.

You leap out of the boat onto the jetty and make your way to the burnt-out shells of the houses. Sitting amongst the ruins are women and old men.

"What happened here?" you demand.

"Come with me," says one of the villagers. "I will take you to the elders and they will tell you all."

With a heavy heart you and your crew follow the old man.

**Now turn to section 1.**

# 1

The elders are sitting down by the shore. After exchanging greetings, you ask, "Who is responsible for this?"

"Kalf, Blood-drinker," replies Erik Redhair.

You shudder. Kalf, Blood-drinker, is the pirate chieftain of the Dragon Ship, *Fenrir*. He is known throughout the Viking world as a destroyer of villages and taker of lives. There are also stories that he drinks the blood of his slaughtered enemies.

"He and his men landed two days ago," continues Erik. "He killed many of our men and took all our goods before setting fire to the village." Erik looks you in the eye. "Will you and your men hunt down Kalf and revenge this death and destruction?"

You think very carefully. This will be a dangerous and difficult quest.

**If you do not wish to risk your life, go to 19.**
**If you agree to do as Erik asks, go to 11.**

## 2

Ignoring your men, you throw yourself overboard in an effort to save yourself. As you swim towards the safety of the rocks, one of the Kraken's many tentacles curls around your waist, gripping you tightly.

You struggle to free yourself, but it is useless. The creature's hold is too strong. Slowly you are pulled downwards into the black depths of the sea. You are no hero; your cowardly action has cost you your life.

**Your adventure has ended. If you wish to begin again, turn back to 1.**

# 3

"We sail northwards until we reach the rocks of the Kraken," you say.

There is a gasp from the crew. "The home of the Kraken?" asks Kimi. "Many ships have been pulled under the sea by that monster."

"Another story to frighten children," you laugh. "Set sail! We head north!"

**Go to 36.**

# 4

When you wake up, you find yourself lying on the floor in a large timber hall.

Several men are standing over you. They are all holding swords.

"He is awake," says one of them. "Tell Kalf."

You sit up. "Where are my men?"

"In Valhalla," says the man. "As you will be when you meet the Blood-drinker!" The others laugh.

After some minutes there is a noise outside and a huge man steps through the doorway.

Your blood turns cold. It is Kalf.

"So this is my enemy," he growls. "Why did you come here?"

"To avenge my people by sending you to the underworld," you say.

"A brave, but foolish venture." Kalf laughs. "But my men have told me that you are fearless in a battle. I have need of men like you, will you submit to me and become one of my warriors?"

**If you decide to join with Kalf, go to 26.**
**If you don't wish to, go to 29.**

## 5

"Head west," you tell Kimi.

A sea mist shrouds your boat as your men pull on the oars, sending your ship gliding through the dark water.

Perfect, you think, Kalf will not see us.

You continue to row, unseen through the wispy mist. Suddenly the mist breaks up to reveal a dragonship heading towards you!

It is Kalf's ship, *Fenrir*!

**If you wish to fight the ship, go to 37.**

**If you wish to try and lose the ship in the mist, go to 47.**

# 6

"We should search the stonghold," you say.

But before you can say anything else, one of Kalf's men appears from the hall. He sees you and begins to shout an alarm.

Within seconds, dozens of Kalf's warriors charge from the hall, screaming blood-freezing battlecries.

You and your men fight bravely, but you are outnumbered. You feel a blow to the head and drop to your knees. Looking up through half closed eyes, you see a sword being raised above your head. But before it can fall, a voice cuts in. "No! Take him to Kalf."

Then you pass into unconsciousness.

**Go to 4.**

# 7

You stand on the prow of the ship and order your men to row slowly.

As you are about to pass between the rocks of the Kraken, you see a small wave breaking ahead of you.

**If you wish to you continue your course, go to 33.**

**If you wish to order your men to stop rowing, go to 27.**

# 8

"Head for the north of the island," you say.

Soon you round a headland and see a bay with a fishing village.

**If you wish to head for the fishing village, go to 20.**

**If you wish to avoid the village and head across the island in search of Kalf, go to 23.**

# 9

The Kraken's huge eye stares at you, causing you to shudder with fear. One of its tentacles slithers across the deck towards you.

You look around and see a spear and an axe within your reach. You have to make an immediate decision; do you pick up the axe and slash at the Kraken's tentacle or hurl the spear into the creature's eye?

**If you wish to use the axe, go to 40.**
**If you wish to use the spear, go to 22.**

# 10

You wait all day, carefully watching Kalf's men. You identify their guard-house and make plans for your attack. One thing puzzles you – there is no sign of any villagers.

Finally night falls and you begin to make your way towards the village.

As you reach the outskirts of the settlement you hear a shout. "Invaders! Enemies!"

A guard has seen you and begins to run away, shouting out more warnings. You chase after him and with a swipe of your axe, silence his cries.

But the noise has alerted Kalf's men. They charge out of the guard-house and the battle begins!

**Go to 13.**

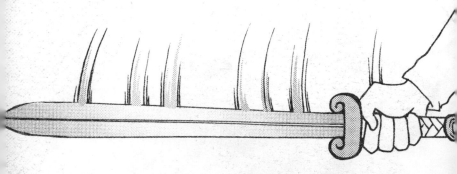

# 11

"We will hunt down Kalf and make him pay," you say. "And if we die in the attempt, then we will all meet again in Valhalla, the hall of slain heroes!" Your men cheer.

Erik shakes your hand and thanks you. He tells you that Kalf will have returned to his island fortress of Stangar.

"Come men, we will avenge our people," you tell your crew.

As you move away, an old man called Hagar steps forward. "Be careful," he warns. "The sea around the island is red from the blood of the warriors who have failed in their attempts to kill the Blood-drinker."

"A sea of blood!" you laugh. "Hagar, these are stories told to scare children…"

"No, you must listen to me," he insists.

**If you wish to listen, go to 46.**

**If you don't think you have the time, go to 38.**

# 12

Your men pull hard on the oars. You take hold of the rudder with Kimi. It takes all your strength to hold a straight course avoiding the centre of the whirlpool and the rocks.

Slowly your ship pulls free of the whirlpool. You sigh with relief and your men collapse, exhausted, onto their oars.

**Go to 17.**

## 13

The fight is over quickly. You and your men easily overpower Kalf's men and send their souls to Valhalla. As you stand amongst the bodies of the dead, several people emerge from the wooden houses.

Your men raise their weapons.

"No!" you order. "These people are harmless villagers."

An elderly man steps forward and asks you who you are and what brings you to their village. You tell them you are here to end the days of Kalf, Blood-drinker.

The villagers cheer. "We have spent many years under the Blood-drinker's evil rule," says the man. "We have to do what he says otherwise we suffer terribly. We will help you to defeat him."

Kimi whispers in your ear. "Can we trust them?" he asks.

**If you wish to take up the villagers' offer of help, go to 45.**

**If you don't trust them, go to 18.**

# 14

Kalf's men form a circle around you. One of his warriors gives you a sword.

You hold on to it tightly and advance on Kalf. "Prepare to die, Blood-drinker."

Kalf swings his sword but you parry his blow.

"Very good," says Kalf. "It is almost a pity that you have to die."

The fight continues. Your attacks come to nothing. Kalf is stronger than you. Then he begins to press forward.

His attack is ferocious. His sword smashes against yours and your blade breaks in two. The force of the blow sends you reeling to the ground.

**If you wish to surrender, go to 26.**

**If you wish to fight on, go to 43.**

# 15

"We haven't time to waste," you tell Karl. "Fix the mast with a rope."

Karl does as you ask and soon your ship pulls away from the shore.

**Go to 42.**

# 16

You address your men. "Vikings, prepare to avenge our people."

They cheer and you charge, waving your weapons in the air and giving blood-chilling cries.

But in the daylight, your attack has no element of surprise. Kalf's warriors are ready for you. You swing your battleaxe, but it is hopeless. You are surrounded. You feel a sharp pain in your side and scream Odin's name. The black hand of death pulls you away.

**Your adventure has ended. If you wish to begin again, turn back to 1.**

# 17

Your ship is suddenly swamped by a huge wave breaking over the ship's bow.

You gasp in horror as several giant tentacles burst from the water, gripping your ship. Your men scream in terror. It is the Kraken! Its monstrous squid-like form emerges from the depths, rocking your boat. Tentacles pull some of your men from the ship and into the water.

**If you wish to fight the Kraken, go to 9.**

**If you wish to abandon your ship and try to reach the rocks, go to 2.**

## 18

"We have come this far without help," you tell the old man. "The gods are on our side and we will defeat Kalf."

You order your men to head across the moors of Stangar to Kalf's stronghold. It is hard going, but you are driven by your desire to avenge your people.

After several hours of travelling, you reach a hill overlooking Kalf's stronghold. You decide to wait for nightfall to attack.

**Go to 39.**

## 19

You shake your head. "I am a trader, not a warrior. Kalf, Blood-drinker is too powerful."

"Yours is the only ship left," says Erik. "Your men will follow you. The Blood-drinker must be sent to hell, where he can cause no more suffering."

**If you wish to change your mind and hunt Kalf, go to 11.**

**If you do not wish to hunt Kalf, go to 30.**

## 20

You land west of the fishing village and disembark from your ship. You and your men head towards the village, being as quiet as you can.

However, as you near the settlement, you see that it is guarded by a group of Kalf's warriors.

**If you wish to fight them now, go to 16.**
**If you wish to wait until nightfall, go to 10.**

## 21

As your ship passes by the rocks, it begins to speed up and swing around to the left.

"Kimi, watch your steering!" you shout.

"It isn't me," replies Kimi.

As your ship begins to spin about, you realise what is happening. You are caught in a deadly whirlpool!

How will you break free of the danger?

**If you order your men to row hard, go to 12.**

**If you order your men to lower the sail, go to 44.**

# 22

You pick up the spear and hurl it into the very centre of the Kraken's eye.

There is a moment's pause: then the air is filled with demonic screaming as the creature thrashes about in pain. Its tentacles flail across the deck causing the boat to rock wildly. Water crashes over the deck. It is only a matter of time before the creature sinks your ship. What should you do now?

**If you wish to rally your men to fight, go to 32.**
**If you want to abandon the fight and save yourself, go to 2.**

## 23

You land away from the village and head up the cliff and onto the high moors of Stangar. It is hard going, but you are driven by your desire to avenge your people.

After several hours of travelling, you reach a hill overlooking a harbour and Kalf's stronghold.

**If you wish to attack now, go to 16.**
**If you wish to wait for nightfall, go to 39.**

## 24

You return to the village. Whilst the mast is being replaced, you and your men gather more food and weapons for the voyage and fight ahead.

Next day as the sun is rising, your longship pulls away from the shore.

"In which direction are we headed?" asks Kimi, your helmsman.

**Did you listen to Hagar's advice? If you did, go to 3.**
**If you didn't, go to 49.**

## 25

"Lower the sail, men," you order. "We don't want Kalf to know that we are coming."

Your men obey then begin to row towards the island.

"Where shall we land?" asks Kimi.

**If you wish to head north, go to 8.**
**If you wish to head west, go to 5.**

## 26

"I submit," you say.

"Hah! You weakling," bellows Kalf. "I thought you had honour in your blood. To surrender when your men have died fighting… I have no need for men like you!"

He raises his sword. Your last sight in this world is the firelight glinting on the blade as it heads towards you. You feel a searing pain in your chest, then the world turns to black…

**Your adventure has ended. If you wish to begin again, turn back to 1.**

## 27

Your ship slows down. Ahead of you is a line of deadly, jagged rocks sticking out of the sea. If you had gone on, your ship would have been ripped to pieces.

**If you wish to steer right, go to 17.**
**If you wish to steer left, go to 21.**

## 28

Kimi sets a course eastwards. You sail on slowly. Your men are too exhausted to row.

A mist falls, shrouding the sea in a white veil. Suddenly from out of the mist a Viking dragonship appears! It is *Fenrir*, Kalf's ship and it is heading for you. You hear the blood-chilling cries of Kalf's men.

"Vikings, row for your lives!" you shout.

But it is useless – your men are too tired. *Fenrir* gains on you. You see Kalf's men preparing to attack.

You and your men take up your weapons, ready to do battle.

**Go to 37.**

## 29

"I will never join you, Blood-drinker," you say defiantly.

"Then you will die…" he moves towards you, sword raised.

You laugh. "So, it is true! You are no man of honour. To kill a defenceless man…"

Your remark stings Kalf. "What do you propose?" he asks.

"I challenge you to mortal combat. Your sword against mine. If I defeat you, then your men will swear allegiance to me… Or are you a coward?"

Kalf thinks for a moment. "Very well." He takes a knife from his belt and cuts his palm. "I swear this blood oath: if you kill me, then my men will swear allegiance to you. And not only that – my gold and jewels will be yours!"

**Go to 14.**

# 30

"I am sorry, I am no hero," you reply. "I do not wish to die."

There is a shout. "By Odin! You are a coward! You are not worthy to live!"

You turn to see one of your men rushing towards you with his sword drawn.

Before you can do anything, you feel a searing pain in your belly. Dropping to your knees, you look up. The last sight you will see in this world is a sword dripping with your blood.

**Your adventure has ended. If you wish to begin again, turn back to 1.**

# 31

As your ship arrives at the quay, you see a group of armed men coming from the houses, heading your way.

"Fight for your lives, Vikings!" you shout. You and your men scramble out of the boat onto the quay. However, you quickly realise that the quay was not a good place to land – there is little room to move and fight. You are trapped!

Kalf's men are soon upon you, screaming oaths and battle cries.

You and your men fight bravely and kill many of Kalf's warriors, but you are outnumbered. You feel a blow to the head and pass into unconsciousness.

**Go to 4.**

## 32

You grasp the battleaxe and hack at another tentacle, but the Kraken continues to attack. You realise that you cannot defeat the creature on your own.

"Vikings!" you shout. "Stand with me! Attack!"

Your men slash at the Kraken's tentacles with their swords and axes. The creature's blood spurts out, mixing with the sea and turning it red.

The Kraken's attention turns to your men. You seize the chance to climb on the side of the boat. With a mighty roar, you swing your battleaxe into the Kraken's head and the creature falls back into the sea, dead.

**Go to 48.**

## 33

As you speed through the water there is a terrible crunching sound and your ship stops dead. The waves were breaking over jagged rocks.

Your ship's hull is torn to pieces. Water pours in. Your men scream angrily at you as your ship sinks into the icy black depths. The rocks of the Kraken have claimed another victim.

**Your adventure has ended. If you wish to begin again, turn back to 1.**

## 34

"We go on," you shout as the storm rages about you.

Your men plead with you to turn back, but you refuse. Suddenly a huge wave hits the ship. There is a loud cracking sound as the mast snaps in half and crashes down on to you, sending you to oblivion.

**Your adventure has ended. If you wish to begin again, turn back to 1.**

## 35

As you sail west the wind is with you and you make good progress through day and night.

"The gods are looking favourably on us," you tell your men. "We will soon be crossing metal with Kalf!"

As dawn breaks, you are proved correct. In the distance lies an island. The rising sun colours it blood-red.

"Stangar," you whisper.

**Go to 25.**

## 36

The days pass as you sail northwards.

After another night of hard rowing, dawn breaks to reveal two huge black rocks, jutting out of the sea.

"The rocks of the Kraken!" you cry. Your men look worried. This place has a bad reputation. The spray from the sea and the mist adds to the gloom.

You have to make a decision about the course you will take to pass the rocks of the Kraken. Will you sail by the left or the right of the rocks, or between them?

**To take the left-hand course, go to 21.**
**To take the right-hand course, go to 17.**
**To sail through the middle, go to 7.**

*Fenrir* pulls alongside and Kalf's men leap across onto the deck of your ship.

The battle is fierce as you and your crew fight bravely. You kill several of Kalf's warriors with your mighty battleaxe. However, the odds are too great. One by one your men fall, until you are the only man left standing.

With a defiant cry you charge forward. An axe strikes you, dropping you to your knees. You look up. The last sight you will see in this world is one of Kalf's warriors grinning wildly.

**If you wish to begin your adventure again, turn back to 1.**

## 38

You hurry back to your ship.

Karl Thornbeard, the ship's carpenter, has bad news. "The mast is damaged," he tells you. "It will need to be replaced before we set sail. I can make a temporary repair but I would rather have a new mast to make sure it doesn't break at sea."

"How long will that take?" you ask.

"A day to replace the mast. Two hours to make a temporary repair."

**If you wish to replace the whole mast, go to 24.**

**If you wish to make a temporary repair, go to 15.**

## 39

You hide amongst the rocks overlooking Kalf's stronghold and wait.

As night falls you are fully rested, so you gather your men together. "Prepare to fight, men!" you say. "For the honour of our people!"

Your men cheer and you charge down the hill towards Kalf's stronghold.

However, warned by your cries, a group of armed warriors pour out from the buildings.

The battle begins. Metal strikes metal; metal strikes flesh.

You and your men fight bravely, causing many casualties. Some of your men are killed, but you force the enemy back into the stronghold. However just as victory seem to be yours, you are stunned by a blow to the head and pass into unconsciousness.

**Go to 4.**

# 40

You pick up the battleaxe and hack at the Kraken's tentacle. The blade slices into the flesh. However, this only enrages the creature.

More tentacles emerge from the sea, slithering over the deck towards you. You chop wildly at the clutching tentacles, but there are too many. You are soon caught in the creature's deadly grip and feel yourself being dragged towards the side of the ship.

You try to break free, but it is no use. You are pulled, screaming, into the gaping blackness of the Kraken's jaws.

**Your adventure has ended. If you wish to begin again, turn back to 1.**

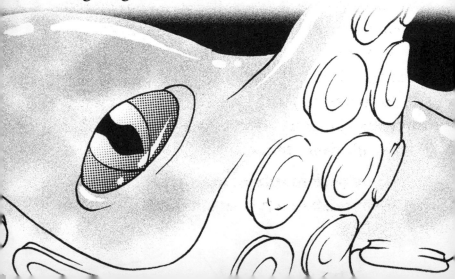

# 41

"We will attack now," you tell your men.

With a bloodcurdling cry you and your men charge into the great hall. You see dozens of men sitting at a large wooden table, eating and drinking. You have taken them by surprise! Your battleaxe is soon red with the blood of Kalf's warriors. However, Kalf's men fight back. You quickly realise that you are outnumbered. One by one your men and the brave villagers fall to the Blood-drinker's warriors.

You continue to fight bravely, but it is hopeless. Before very long you are the last man standing. You swing your battleaxe, but it is smashed from your grasp. Kalf's men move in for the kill. But before you too can join your men in Valhalla there is a cry of "Enough!"

A huge man steps through the throng of warriors. It is Kalf!

He looks at you with blazing eyes. "I need fighters like you. Will you join with me and swear allegiance to me?"

**If you wish to submit to Kalf, go to 26.**
**If you wish to refuse to join him, go to 29.**

## 42

Within hours of leaving your village, a sea-storm breaks out. The wind and rain rip at your sail and your ship is tossed about on the waves.

"The mast won't hold up," says Karl. "We must return home!"

**If you want to carry on, go to 34.**

**If you give the order to return home, go to 24.**

## 43

Kalf raises his sword and brings it down with a mighty cry. As he does so, you roll away and thrust your broken sword upwards. The blade enters Kalf's chest. He stares at you in disbelief.

**Go to 50.**

## 44

Your men leave their oars and stow the sails, but the force of the whirlpool is too strong! Your ship spins around wildly and some of the crew are flung out into the icy black waters.

The last sound you hear is the roar of the sea and the cries of your men as you too are sucked into the watery depths.

**Your adventure has ended. If you wish to begin again, turn back to 1.**

# 45

"We would value your help," you tell the villagers.

"We can show you a secret way into Kalf's stronghold," the old man says.

You thank him and set off with your men and some of the younger villagers across the moors of Stangar, towards Kalf's stronghold.

The sun has long set when you arrive at your destination.

"Now we take the path to a secret entrance," says one of the villagers.

You and your men follow the villagers down a steep slope into a mass of gorse and thick brambles. You cut your way through and soon find yourselves inside Kalf's stronghold.

You hear a roar of laughter from within one of the great timber buildings. "That is Kalf's great hall. He will be feasting with his men," says a villager. "You should attack now."

**If you wish to attack straight away, go to 41.**

**If you wish to look around the stronghold, go to 6.**

# 46

"I have knowledge of Kalf's island," says the old man. "You must sail north for three days where you will find the rocks of the Kraken. Then turn westwards for a further day. There you will find Stangar."

You thank Hagar for his advice.

**Now go to 38.**

# 47

"Head back into the mist!" you tell your men. They obey and soon your ship is hidden in the white blanket.

You order your men to stop rowing and the ship drifts silently through the mist – there is no sight or sound of *Fenrir*.

Eventually the mist clears and you see a small fishing village. A small wooden quay juts out into the sea.

**If you wish to land at the quay, go to 31.**

**If you wish to land away from the village and head off in search of Kalf's stronghold, go to 23.**

## 48

The Kraken has been defeated, but at a cost. Your men sit exhausted and bleeding.

"We have lost seven men," says Kimi. "And the ship is damaged. Should we go on?"

"Yes. We carry on," you say. "Kalf has to be stopped. Steer a new course."

**If you wish to head east, go to 28.**
**If you wish to head west, go to 35.**

## 49

"We will head south," you tell Kimi. "Perhaps we will find Stangar there."

Kimi pulls on the rudder oar and sets a course southward.

Many hours pass. The weather is turning for the worse. The sky is black as a raven and the sea is getting rougher. Soon the waves are crashing at your ship.

"We should turn around or the storm will sink us," cries Kimi.

**If you turn northwards, go to 36.**
**If you wish to brave the coming storm, go to 34.**

Kalf's sword slips from his blood-soaked hand. He feels the Valkyrie's death grip pulling him into the afterlife. "Honour my blood oath," he orders his men, then falls to the floor, dead.

You stand and raise your bloody, broken sword above your head. Kalf's men throw down their weapons and pledge their allegiance.

You have defeated the Blood-drinker and avenged your people. Kalf's gold will pay for your village to be rebuilt and you will be able to return to your home as a hero!

If you enjoyed reading

# Viking Blood

there are more titles in the
I Hero series:

## Death or Glory!

## Gorgon's Cave

## Code Mission

978 0 7496 7664 3

978 0 7496 7666 7

978 0 7496 7667 4

# Death or Glory!

Steve Barlow and Steve Skidmore

Illustrated by Sonia Leong

You are a warrior living on the island of Britannia – today called Great Britain.

It is almost 37 years since the Romans invaded Britannia. Their forces have conquered most of the country.

You are part of a tribe locked in a bitter struggle with the Romans. You have already proved your bravery by leading many daring raids against the armies of Rome, burning their camps and driving them back from your lands.

But now, a powerful Roman army has arrived and it is about to attack your stronghold. If they win, Britain will become a Roman province. Any Britons who survive the battle will be captured and sold as slaves.

You are sharpening your sword in readiness for the battle when you are called to a meeting with the chief of your tribe.

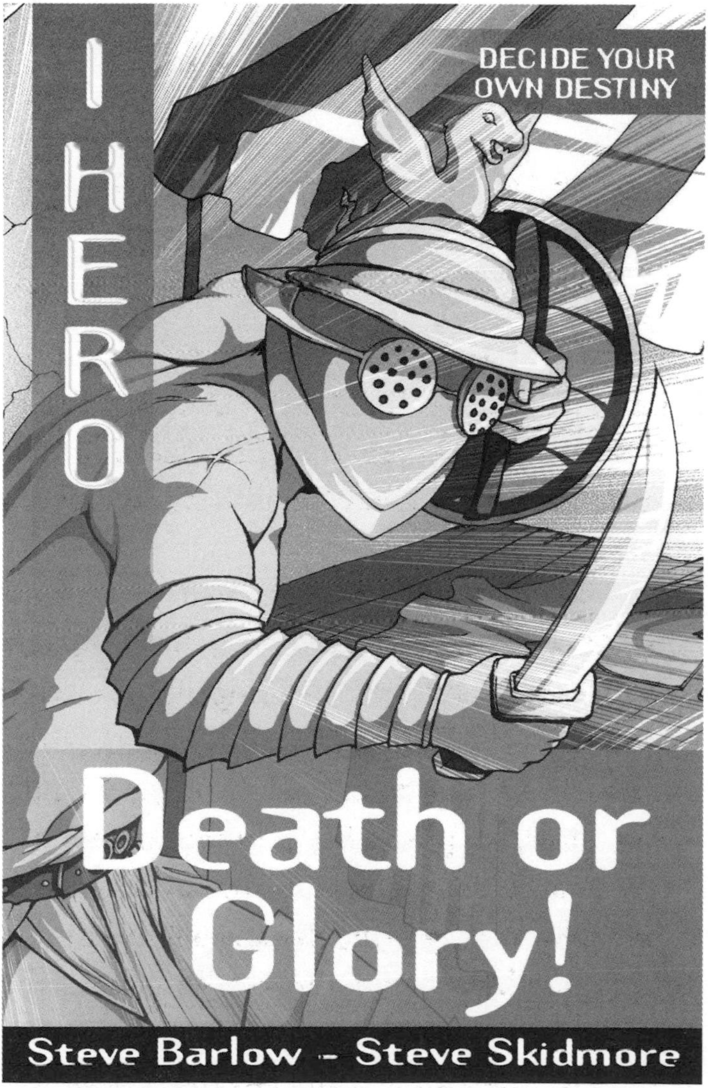
I HERO
DECIDE YOUR OWN DESTINY
Death or Glory!
Steve Barlow - Steve Skidmore